Amelia Jane

Gets into Trouble

Seven stories from
More about Amelia Jane!

Enid Blyton

Illustrated by Rene Cloke

Beaver Books

The stories in this book were taken from the collection
More About Amelia Jane!
First published in 1954
Revised edition published in 1974 by Dean & Son Limited
52–54 Southwark Street, London SE1 1VA

This paperback edition published in 1978 by
The Hamlyn Publishing Group Limited
London · New York · Sydney · Toronto
Astronaut House, Feltham, Middlesex, England
Reprinted 1979

© Copyright Enid Blyton 1954
© Copyright Darrell Waters Limited 1969
ISBN 0 600 30406 X

Printed in England by
Cox & Wyman Limited
London, Reading and Fakenham
Set in Monotype Baskerville

Contents

1 Amelia Jane gets into trouble

Amelia Jane, as you all know, is a very clever and very naughty doll. The toys could never keep pace with her tricks – but one day she got herself into trouble.

It happened like this. Billy came into the nursery and looked round for his Red-Indian doll. 'Redskin, where are you?' he said. 'I'm going to take you out to tea with me this afternoon and I'm going in *my* Red-Indian things, too! We're going to play with Betty and Dick, and they're going to dress up as Red Indians as well. So, with you, we'll be four Red Indians! We'll have fun!'

He began looking for Redskin, the doll dressed up as a fine little Red Indian.

But before he could find him his mother called out. 'Billy! Come here a minute. I want you.'

Billy ran out. Amelia Jane sat up, her eyes gleaming. 'Redskin, don't you go! They might even cut off your head.'

'That's dreadful!' said Redskin, in alarm. Although he was dressed as a fierce Red Indian Brave, he wasn't at all brave really. 'Oh dear! I don't want to go. I really don't!'

'Well, I'll go instead,' said Amelia Jane, in a kind voice. 'I'll do you a good turn and put on your clothes and go instead of you. Would you like that?'

'Oh, yes!' said Redskin. He stripped off his Red Indian clothes, and took off his magnificent head-dress of gay feathers that fell right down his back to his feet.

Amelia Jane dressed herself up in them. My word, she did look grand! You should have seen her! She pranced about, her feathers flying behind her, looking very

8

smart in leather trousers with fringes down them, and the head-dress on her black hair. 'I'm grand! I'm fierce! I'm going to hit people with my axe!'

She had a little chopper that went with Redskin's clothes. She began to rush at the toys, pretending to chop them. They didn't like it at all.

'Now stop that, Amelia Jane!' said the sailor doll. 'And take off those clothes. You know perfectly well that nobody will chop off Redskin's head if he goes out to tea — you've only said that because you want to dress up and prance about pretending to be a Red Indian. Take those clothes off.'

But all that Amelia Jane did was to rush at the golliwog and the sailor doll, and pretend to chop off their heads. They were very cross indeed — but Amelia was bigger than they were, and it was difficult to stop her.

In rushed Billy. He caught hold of Amelia Jane, thinking she was Redskin, his Red-Indian doll. Out of the door he went at top speed, calling out, 'I'm ready, Mother! I'm just coming!'

Amelia Jane planned to have a wonderful time. She would go stalking Betty and Dick with Billy. She would take them prisoner. She would chop at them, with the little chopper. My goodness, Amelia Jane was going to have the time of her life!

But it didn't turn out quite like that. Billy, Betty and Dick got the gardener to hide Amelia Jane somewhere, so that they could stalk her and pounce on her and take her prisoner!

So Amelia was put into the middle of a bush by the gardener, and left there. The children began to hunt for her, going along in single file, leaping high in the air, and filling the garden with terrifying war-whoops.

Amelia Jane shivered in the bush. How she hoped they wouldn't find her. She didn't mind stalking the others and pouncing on them – but she didn't want to be pounced on and taken prisoner herself!

Well, the children soon found her. They surrounded the bush, and Betty yelled out loudly: 'The enemy is hiding here! I see him! Pounce, brothers, pounce!'

And they all pounced! Amelia Jane was pulled roughly from the bush and thrown to the ground.

'You're our prisoner!' yelled the three,

and chopped all round her with their wooden choppers. They didn't even touch Amelia, but she thought they were going to every time a chopper came down – biff, bang!

'Let's tie him to a tree and dance round him before we shoot him,' said Billy. So they took Amelia and tied her to a little tree.

'Funny sort of doll, this,' said Dick, looking closely at her. 'He's got a face more like a girl-doll than a boy-doll. WOWOO-WOW!'

That was another war-shout, yelled right in poor Amelia's ear. She was so scared that she nearly cried.

'Now he's tied up. He can't get away. He's our prisoner,' said Betty. 'Let's get our bows and arrows and shoot at him. Wangity-whang!'

But fortunately for Amelia Jane, before they could get their bows and arrows, the tea-bell rang loudly, and the three fierce

Red Indians raced up to the house in glee.

Amelia Jane began to sob. She struggled with the knots that tied her, but they were tight and she couldn't undo even one of them. She was very frightened. Would the three children really shoot her with arrows? She was only a doll, so they might. How she wished she hadn't been silly enough to make Redskin give her his clothes!

'I'm always doing silly things!' wept Amelia. 'I wish I didn't. Oh, what shall I do?'

She waited for the children to come back. She waited and she waited. But they didn't come. Betty's mother had said she thought it was going to rain, so they could either play a *quiet* game of Red Indians indoors, or a noisy game of snap, whichever they liked.

They chose snap, and forgot all about Amelia Jane, tied to the tree in the garden. In fact Billy forgot about her completely,

13

and even went home without her! So there she was when darkness came, still tied up tightly, jumping in fright every time an owl came by and hooted.

The toys were surprised when Billy came home without Amelia Jane. He didn't say anything about leaving her behind until just before he went to bed. He was sitting in his pyjamas eating his supper in the nursery with his sister, when he suddenly gave a cry.

'What's the matter?' said his mother.

'It's Redskin. I've forgotten to bring him home,' said Billy. 'We tied him up to a tree to shoot arrows at him, and then we went in to tea and I forgot all about him. He's still there, poor thing. And it's dark and rainy. Mother, I must go and get him.'

'No, you mustn't,' said his mother, firmly. 'You are certainly not going to run down the dark rainy street in your pyjamas. You can get Redskin tomorrow. If he's under a tree he won't get very wet.'

'But he'll be frightened,' said Billy. 'He won't like it.'

'Well, that's your fault,' said Mother. 'When we forget things we often make others suffer as well as ourselves. You should have remembered to bring Redskin home.'

Now, of course, the toys couldn't help hearing all this, because they were sitting round the nursery watching the children eat their supper. They were full of horror.

What! Amelia Jane tied up to a tree, left alone in the darkness and the rain! Naughty as she was, and cross as they felt with her, they were very sorry. When the children had gone to bed they got together in a corner and talked about it.

'I'll go and rescue her,' said Redskin, bravely. 'I know the way. I've been to that house before.'

'But you haven't got any clothes on,' said the sailor doll. 'You'll get soaked. And it's frightening to go out in the dark at

15

night. You might meet a fierce dog or a yowling cat who would pounce on you. Anyway, you're not very brave.'

'Oh, I know that,' said Redskin, sadly. 'It's a pity to have to be a Redskin doll and not feel brave. That's really why I'm going. I'm not brave, in fact I'm very frightened, but I feel I *ought* to be brave, so I'm going to rescue Amelia.'

'Well, that's very nice of you, after she tricked you into taking off your clothes and letting her go out to tea instead of you,' said the golliwog, patting Redskin on the back. 'All right, you go then, if you know the way. What about clothes? There's a little oil-skin cape and hat in the doll's wardrobe. You could borrow those.'

So Redskin put them on and he looked rather queer, not at all like a Redskin doll! Then he slipped out of the window, climbed down the tree outside and set off in the darkness to Betty's house.

The rain hit him on the nose, and ran

16

down his oil-skin coat in little rivers. It went down his neck, too, because his hat didn't fit very well. At last he came to the garden of Betty's house and slipped through a hole in the fence.

Amelia Jane was still tied to the tree. An owl had hooted in her ear. A spider had walked over her face. A hedgehog had walked so near that his spines pricked her legs. She was lonely and scared.

She heard a noise. What was that? Oh, what was that? It sounded like someone coming nearer and nearer, creeping through the bushes! Amelia began to tremble and shake.

'Who is it? Go away! Leave me alone! Oh, don't come near me, I'm scared, I'm frightened! Don't frighten me any more. Go away, whoever it is!'

But the footsteps came nearer and nearer, and then a head poked round a bush. Amelia Jane gave a scream.

'Go away! I'm frightened of you!'

Well, it was Redskin, of course, come to rescue her! 'It's all right,' he said. 'It's only me, Redskin. I'll undo your knots, Amelia Jane.'

Amelia could have hugged him! Dear, dear Redskin! Oh, how could she have tricked him like that! She would always love him now.

He undid the knots. She stretched herself stiffly and then sneezed. 'Let's hurry home,' said Redskin. 'You've caught cold. I'll lead the way.'

Well, it wasn't long before they were both back in the nursery again, leaving little wet marks all over the floor. As soon as they got there Amelia Jane flung herself on Redskin and hugged him so hard that he squealed.

'Good, kind, *brave* Redskin! Oh, what courage you've got! Oh, how plucky you are! Toys, Redskin is quite the bravest toy in the nursery!'

Redskin could hardly believe his ears when all the toys crowded round and thumped him on the back, and said the same as Amelia! 'But I'm not brave!' he kept saying. 'I never have been! I was frightened all the time. Brave people aren't frightened.'

'The bravest people of all are those who are frightened and yet go on being brave,' said the sailor doll, helping him off with his oil-skin coat. 'Amelia Jane has no right to wear a Red Indian's clothes – she's a little coward! As soon as they are dry, you must

19

wear them again, because you really and truly are a RED INDIAN BRAVE!'

The toys dried Redskin's clothes, as soon as Amelia Jane had taken them off. Amelia dressed humbly in her own clothes. She felt ashamed of herself. She sneezed loudly.

'I'm getting a dreadful cold,' she said, very sorry for herself.

'It serves you right,' said the sailor doll. 'Don't sneeze all over us, please. We're giving a party for Redskin soon, and you'd better not come in case you give everyone your cold.'

So now Amelia Jane is sitting by herself in a corner sneezing into her hanky, watching the most wonderful party going on, given for Redskin, the Red-Indian doll. Nobody feels at all sorry for her. I don't know if you do?

Billy's going to be very surprised to-morrow to find that Redskin is sitting in the nursery instead of tied up to the tree! He's going to puzzle about that for days.

20

2 Now then, Amelia Jane!

Amelia Jane, the big naughty doll in the nursery, was doing a bit of sewing. She sat in the corner, her head bent over her work, sewing away.

'Aha! So you've decided to sew on that shoe button at last!' said the clockwork clown, coming up. 'Quite time, too – your shoe's fallen off heaps of times!'

'You be quiet,' said Amelia Jane.

'And while you're about it, why not mend that hole in your frock?' said a wooden skittle, hopping up. 'Or do you *like* holes in your dress, Amelia Jane?'

'You be quiet, too,' said Amelia, and jabbed at him with her needle. He hopped away with a chuckle.

He was soon back again. 'And what about your right sock?' he said. 'It's got a great big hole in the heel. And what about . . .?'

Amelia Jane jabbed at him again so hard that the thimble flew off her finger. It rolled away over the floor into a corner.

'Bother you, skittle!' said Amelia Jane, in a temper. 'Now you go and pick up that thimble and bring it back to me! Why do you tease me like this? I don't like you.'

'Shan't pick up your thimble!' said the skittle, enjoying himself. 'Silly old Amelia Jane!'

'Stop yelling at one another, and you go and pick up the thimble, skittle,' said the teddy bear, crossly. 'Can't you see I'm trying to read?'

The skittle didn't dare to disobey the big fat bear. He had once been rude to the bear and the bear had sat on him for a whole day, and the skittle hadn't liked that at all. The bear was so heavy.

So he picked up the thimble – but he didn't give it back to Amelia Jane. No – he put it on his head for a hat! Then he walked up and down in a very silly way, saying, 'Look at my new hat! Oh, *do* look at my new hat!'

Everybody looked, of course, and all the toys laughed at the skittle because he really did look funny in a thimble-hat.

He took it off and bowed to them, and then put it back again.

'*Will* you give me my thimble?' cried Amelia Jane, in a rage. 'Give it to me AT ONCE!'

'Say "please", Amelia,' said the bear. 'You sound very rude.'

'I *shan't* say "please"!' cried Amelia. 'And don't you interfere. Skittle, if you don't give me back my thimble at once I'll chase you and knock you over!'

'Can't catch *me*! Can't catch *me*!' said the skittle, who was really being very funny and very annoying. He ran here and there, and he kept taking his thimble-hat on and off to Amelia in a very ridiculous way.

Well, Amelia Jane wasn't going to let a skittle be cheeky to her, so up she got. She raced after the skittle, and he rushed away. But Amelia Jane caught him – and do you know what she did? Instead of taking the thimble off his head, she banged her hand down on it so hard that it went right over the poor skittle's nose, and he couldn't see a thing.

'Oh! Oh, it's so tight now I can't get it off!' yelled the skittle, trying to force the thimble off his head.

Amelia Jane laughed.

'That'll teach you to wear my thimble for a hat and be so rude to me,' she said.

'Help, help!' shouted the skittle. 'It's hurting me! Oooooooooh! Ow! OOOO-OOOOOOH!'

'It really *is* hurting him,' said the bear, getting up. 'Dear, dear – I shall never finish my book today. Stand still, you silly skittle. I'll take the thimble off.'

Well, he tugged and he pulled, and he pulled and he tugged – but he couldn't get that thimble off!

Then the golliwog came up and had a try – but he couldn't get the thimble off either.

Amelia Jane tried – but it wasn't a bit of good; that thimble was jammed so hard on the skittle's head that it really could *not* be moved!

'You'll have to wear the thimble always,' said the bear at last. The skittle lay down and yelled.

'I can't! I don't want to! Take it off, take it off! It's tight, I tell you!'

'We'll simply *have* to do something,' said the golliwog. 'Else the skittle will go on yelling for ever, and I don't think I could bear that.'

'Of *course* something must be done,' said the other skittles, who had popped up, looking very worried. 'Amelia Jane is very naughty.'

'That's nothing new,' said the bear. 'Dear me, do stop yelling, skittle. You'll wake up the household!'

Then the bear thought of something. 'Oh, I've got an idea,' he said. 'What about going out to ask the little black imp who lives in the pansy bed if he knows of a spell to help us. A Get-Loose Spell, perhaps.'

26

'A good idea,' said the golliwog. 'Amelia Jane, go and find the imp and ask him.'

'What! In the middle of a dark night!' said Amelia Jane. 'No, thank you. And anyway, I don't like that imp!'

'Amelia Jane, if you don't go and ask him we shall take your best ribbon and hide it,' said the bear.

'Oh, no, don't do that!' said Amelia. 'It's my party ribbon. All right, you horrid things – I'll go. But I know a very good way of getting the thimble off the skittle.'

'How?' asked the toys.

'Chop off his head!' said Amelia Jane. 'He has so few brains that he'd never even notice his head was gone!'

'We *will* take away your best ribbon now,' said the bear, as the skittle gave a loud yell of fright.

'No, no – I didn't mean it!' said Amelia Jane. 'I'll go this very minute to find the imp.'

Well, off she went, climbing out of the

27

window and down to the pansy bed.

The little black imp was there, wide awake.

'Black imp,' began Amelia, 'I want your help.'

'What will you give me for it?' asked the imp, at once. He didn't like Amelia.

'Nothing,' said Amelia. 'Oh – let go my foot, you horrid little imp!'

'I'm taking your shoe for payment,' said the imp. 'And the other one too. They will fit me nicely. Now, it's no good yelling. I've got them. I've no doubt you've been just as naughty as usual, so it serves you right. Now – what do you want my help for?'

Amelia Jane told him sulkily. 'The skittle is wearing my thimble jammed down hard on his head. How can we get it off?'

'Make the thimble bigger, of course,' said the imp. 'Then his head will be too small for it and it will slip off.'

'But how can we make the thimble bigger?' asked Amelia Jane.

'Easy,' said the imp. 'If you heat any-thing made of metal it becomes just a tiny bit larger – so heat the thimble, Amelia – and it will slip off the skittle's head.'

'But how can we heat it?' said Amelia, not really believing the imp.

'Stand him on his head in hot water,' said the imp. 'You could have thought of that yourself. Now go away. I want to try on your shoes.'

Amelia went back to the nursery. 'The imp says that if we stand the skittle on his head in hot water, the thimble will get a bit larger and slip off,' said Amelia.

'I don't believe a word of it,' said the bear.

'Well, that's what he *said*,' said Amelia. 'He didn't tell me anything else. And I had to give him my shoes for that advice.'

'Hm,' said the golliwog. 'Well, poor old skittle – we'd better try it, anyway. Bear, put a little hot water into the basin, will you? Don't put the plug in in case it gets too deep – just let the water run in and out, and we'll pop the skittle in on his head, and heat the thimble in the water.'

Well, the skittle howled and yelled and kicked up a great fuss, but the bear and the golliwog were very firm with him. They turned him upside down and held him in the hot water, so that the heat warmed up the thimble on his head.

And will you believe it? – the thimble slipped off, just as the imp had said it would. But alas – it rolled round the basin, and disappeared down the plug-hole! It was gone!

'Oh – my thimble, my thimble!' yelled Amelia Jane. But it was gone for good. Nobody ever saw it again.

'Serves you right, Amelia,' said the bear, turning the poor skittle the right way up again. 'Well, who would have thought the imp knew a spell like that? Did *you* know that heat made things just a bit bigger, clockwork clown?'

'I never did,' said the clown.

But the funny thing is that it's *true*! So if ever a thimble gets stuck on one of your skittles you'll know what to do – stand him on his head in hot water and it will slip off!

And now Amelia Jane can't *bear* doing her mending, because she hasn't got a thimble and she pricks her finger all the time. Still, as the toys tell her – it's her own fault!

3 Amelia Jane's boomerang

Amelia Jane found a toy boomerang at the back of the cupboard. Do you know what a boomerang is? It is a bit of curved wood made in such a way that it will always come back to the one who throws it.

You can see the boomerang Amelia Jane found if you look at the picture. She didn't know what it was, at first. Then, when she threw it into the air and found that it came back to her, she was thrilled.

'Now I'll have some fun!' she cried, and she threw the boomerang at the chimneys on the dolls' house! It knocked them off and they slid down the roof, fell to the ground and gave the clockwork mouse a terrible fright.

The boomerang flew back to Amelia Jane, and she caught it. 'Now I'll take off the sailor doll's hat!' she said with a giggle, and threw it again. It neatly took off the sailor doll's hat, and came back to Amelia Jane. She laughed at the sailor doll's look of surprise when he felt his hat knocked off.

'Oh, my goodness! Amelia Jane has found the old boomerang!' said the bear. 'I hid it away. Amelia, give it to me.'

Amelia Jane threw the boomerang at him, and it sliced off the tip of one of his ears, and then flew back to the doll. The bear was very angry.

He ran at Amelia to get the boomerang. But in a trice she flung it at him again and he fell over. The boomerang returned to her hand. She laughed excitedly.

'It's no good! I'm *awfully* good with this. If you come rushing at me I'll throw it at you. So keep away. Now watch – I'm going to throw it at the snapdragons in that vase! I'll chop off some of their heads!'

And that's just what she did! The boomerang flew through the air, hit two snapdragons, broke their pretty heads, and then came flying back to the naughty doll.

Amelia Jane had a lovely time that day. She knocked the little china dog off the mantelpiece with her boomerang, and he fell on to the fender and broke a bit off one paw. She threw it at the little mouse who came for crumbs, and he lost two of his

whiskers. And she threw it at the railway train and cut the funnel right off.

'How can we stop her?' said the clockwork clown in despair. He had had his hat knocked off six times by the boomerang and now he had stuffed it into his pocket for safety.

'I know where the old pop-gun is,' said the pink cat suddenly. 'Shall we get that? It's got a cork on a string, and it always jerks back when it's shot out. You put the cork into the end of the gun, press the trigger – and out shoots the cork. But because it's on a string it always jerks back to the shooter again, like the boomerang goes back to Amelia Jane.'

This was quite a long speech for the pink cat to make, and everyone listened to it, except Amelia Jane, who was trying to knock down a silver thimble left on the mantelpiece.

'Yes! Get the pop-gun!' cried the bear, so the pink cat went to get it. He brought it out of an old box and showed it to the others. The golliwog fitted the cork into the end. It was on a long string tied to the gun. He pressed the trigger.

POP! Out flew the cork quite fiercely, and hit the bear on the right paw. He gave a yell. 'Don't practise on me, silly! That stung! Practise on Amelia Jane!'

The golly grinned. He went over to Amelia Jane and pointed the pop-gun at the back of her head.

POP! The cork flew out, caught her hair-ribbon, and then jerked back on its string.

Amelia Jane got a terrible shock.

'Oh! What was that?' she cried, and swung round at once.

'We've got a boomerang-cork!' grinned the golliwog, and shot at her again. POP! The cork hit her on the nose and she almost fell over.

'Now you stop that!' cried Amelia Jane, 'or I'll throw my boomerang at you!'

'Well, every time you throw your boomerang we're going to shoot you with the pop-gun!' said the golly, putting the cork into the gun again. 'There's no reason why we shouldn't have a bit of fun, too! Look out!'

Pop! The cork hit Amelia Jane right in her middle and she gave a squeal. 'Oh! Oh! You've hit my dinner! Wait till I get that horrid cork! I'll throw it away!'

But she couldn't get the cork because it was tied on with string to the gun, and it always jerked back when it was fired out.

The toys had a wonderful time chasing her round the nursery, popping the cork at her. She didn't have a chance to throw the boomerang at them.

'You're very unkind,' she sobbed as she tried to dodge the toys.

'Oh, no – we're only doing the sort of thing you've been doing,' said the golliwog. 'You give us your boomerang and we'll give you the pop-gun. Then we can each have a

turn at throwing the boomerang too.'

'No,' said Amelia. 'You'd only throw that at me as well. Promise not to and I'll give it to you.'

They promised, and Amelia Jane handed over the boomerang. The golly at once went to hide it away where it would never be found again. But, oh dear, Amelia Jane didn't promise not to shoot at the toys with the pop-gun, and the very first thing she did was to point it at the bear and fire.

POP! It flew out and hit him so hard in his tummy that it made him growl. But she couldn't shoot the cork again because the golly had cut the string and it didn't jerk back to the gun!

'Aha!' said the sailor doll, picking up the loose cork and putting it into his pocket, 'you won't do *that* again, naughty Amelia Jane! Go and stand in the corner till we say you can come out. If you don't, we'll take the gun, tie on the string to the cork and do a bit of shooting again!'

So Amelia Jane is standing in the corner, sulking, and I rather think the toys are going to forget about her for a very long time!

4 Amelia Jane has a good idea

The new teddy bear was very small indeed.
The toys stared at him when he first came
into the playroom, wondering what he was.

'Good gracious! I believe you're a teddy
bear!' said Amelia Jane, the big, naughty
doll. 'I thought you were a peculiar-shaped
mouse.'

'Well, I'm not,' said the small bear,
sharply, and pressed himself in the middle.
'Grrrrrr! Hear me growl? Well, no mouse
can growl. It can only squeak.'

'Yes. You're a bear all right,' said the
golliwog, coming up. 'I hear you've come to
live with us. Well, I'll show you your place
in the toy cupboard – right at the back
there, look.'

'I don't like being at the back, it's too dark,' said the little bear. 'I'll be at the front here, by this big brick-box.'

'Oh, no you won't. That's *my* place when I want to sit in the toy-cupboard,' said Amelia Jane. 'And let me tell you this, small bear – if you live with us you'll have to take on lots of little bits of work. We all do. You'll have to wind up the clockwork clown when he runs down, you'll have to clean the dolls' house windows, and you'll have to help the engine-driver polish his big red train.'

'Dear me, I don't think I want to do any of those things,' said the bear. 'I'm lazy. I don't like working.'

'Well, you'll just have to,' said Amelia Jane. 'Otherwise you won't get any of the biscuit crumbs that the children drop on the floor, you won't get any of the sweets in the toy sweet-shop – and we're allowed some every week – and you won't come to any parties. So there.'

'Pooh!' said the bear and stalked off to pick up some beads out of the bead-box and thread himself a necklace.

'He's vain as well as lazy,' said the golliwog in disgust. 'Hey, bear – what's your name? Or are you too lazy to have one?'

'My name is Sidney Gordon Eustace,' said the bear, haughtily. 'And please remember that I don't like being called Sid.'

'Sid!' yelled all the toys at once, and the bear looked furious. He turned his head away, and went on threading the beads.

'Sidney Gordon Eustace!' said the clown, with a laugh. 'I guess he gave himself those names. No sensible child would ever call a teddy bear that. Huh!'

The bear was not much use in the playroom. He just would *not* do any of the jobs there at all. He went surprisingly deaf when anyone called to him to come and clean or polish or sweep. He would pretend to be asleep, or just walk about humming a little tune as if nobody was calling his name at all. It was most annoying.

'Sidney! Come and shake the mats for the dolls' house dolls!' the golliwog called. No answer came from Sidney at all.

'SIDNEY! Come here! You're not as deaf as all that!'

The bear never even turned his head. 'Hey, Sidney Gordon Eustace – come and do your jobs!' yelled the golliwog. 'SID, SID, SID!'

No answer. 'All right!' shouted the golliwog, angrily. 'You shan't have that nice big crumb of chocolate biscuit we found under the table this morning.'

It was always the same whenever there was a job to be done. 'Sidney, come here!' But Sidney never came. He never did one single thing for any of the toys.

'What are we going to do about him?' said the big teddy bear. 'I'd like to spank him – but he's too quick for me. Amelia Jane – can't you think of a good idea?'

'Oh, yes,' said Amelia at once. 'I know what we'll do. We'll get Sidney-the-mouse to come and do the things that Sidney-the-bear should do – and he shall have all the crumbs and titbits that the bear should have. He won't like that – a common little house-mouse getting all his treats!'

'Dear me – is the house-mouse's name Sidney, too?' said the golliwog in surprise. 'I never knew that before. When we want him we usually go to his hole and shout "Mouse" and he comes.'

'Well, I'll go and shout "Sidney",' said Amelia Jane, 'and you'll see – he'll come!' So she went to the little hole at the bottom of the wall near the book-case and shouted down it.

'Sidney! Sid-Sid-Sidney! We want you!'

The little bear, of course, didn't turn round – *he* wasn't going to come when his name was called. But someone very small came scampering up the passage to the hole-entrance. It was the tiny brown house-

mouse, with bright black eyes and twitch-
ing whiskers.

'Ah, Sidney,' said Amelia Jane. 'Will you
just come and shake the mats in the dolls'
house, please? They are very dusty. We'll
give you a big chocolate biscuit crumb and
a drink of lemonade out of the little teapot
if you will.'

'Can I drink out of the spout?' said the
tiny mouse, pleased. 'I like drinking out of
the spout.'

'Yes, of course,' said Amelia Jane. The
little mouse set about shaking the mats
vigorously, and the job was soon done.

'Isn't Sidney wonderful?' said Amelia in
a loud voice to the others. 'Sidney-the-
mouse, I mean, of course, not silly Sidney-
the-bear. He wouldn't have the strength
to shake mats like that, poor thing. Sidney,
here's your chocolate biscuit crumb and
there's the teapot full of lemonade.'

Sidney the bear didn't like this at all.
Fancy making a fuss of a silly little mouse,

and giving him treats like that. He would very much have liked the crumb and the lemonade himself. He pressed himself in the middle and growled furiously when the mouse had gone.

'Don't have that mouse here again,' he said. 'I don't like hearing somebody else being called Sidney. Anyway, I don't believe his name *is* Sidney. It's not a name for a mouse.'

'Well, for all you know, his name might be Sidney Gordon Eustace just like yours,' said Amelia Jane at once.

'Pooh! Whoever heard of a mouse having a grand name like that?' said the bear.

'Well, next time you won't do a job, we'll call all three names down the hole,' said Amelia, 'and see if the little mouse will answer to them!'

Next night there was going to be a party. Everyone had to help to get ready for it. Amelia Jane called to the little bear.

'Sidney! Come and set the tables for the party. Sidney, do you hear me?'

Sidney did, but he pretended not to, of course. Set party tables! Not he! So he went deaf again, and didn't even turn his head.

'Sidney Gordon Eustace, do as you're told or you won't come to the party,' bawled the big teddy bear in a fine old rage.

The little bear didn't answer. Amelia Jane gave a sudden grin.

'Never mind,' she said. 'We'll get Sidney Gordon Eustace, the little mouse, to come and set the tables. He does them beautifully and never breaks a thing. He can come to the party afterwards then. I'll call him.'

The little bear turned his head. 'He won't answer to *that* name, you know he won't!' he said, scornfully. 'Call away! No mouse ever had a name as grand as mine.'

Amelia Jane went to the mouse-hole and called down it.

'Sidney Gordon Eustace, are you there?' she called. 'If you are at home, come up and help us. Sidney Gordon Eustace, are you there?'

And at once there came the pattering of tiny feet, and with a loud squeak the little mouse peeped out of his hole, his whiskers quivering.

'Ah – you are at home,' said Amelia. 'Well, dear little Sidney, will you set the tables for us? We're going to have a party.'

The mouse was delighted. He was soon at work, and in a short while the four tables were set with tiny table-cloths and china. Then he went to help the dolls' house dolls to cut sandwiches. The bear watched all this out of the corner of his eye. He was quite amazed that the mouse had come when he was called Sidney Gordon Eustace – goodness, fancy a common little mouse owning a name like that!

He was very cross when he saw that the mouse was going to the party. Amelia Jane found him a red ribbon to tie round his neck and one for his long tail. He was given a place at the biggest table, and everyone made a fuss of him.

'Good little Sidney! You do work well! Whatever should we do without you? What will you have to eat?'

The mouse ate a lot. *Much* too much, the little bear thought. He didn't go to the party. He hadn't been asked and he didn't quite like to go because there was no chair for him and no plate. But, oh, all those nice things to eat! *Why* hadn't he been sensible and gone to set the tables?

'Goodnight, Sidney Gordon Eustace,' said Amelia to the delighted mouse. 'We've loved having you.'

Now, after this kind of thing had happened three or four times the bear got tired of it.

He hated hearing people yell for 'Sidney, Sidney!' down the mouse-hole, or to hear the mouse addressed as Sidney Gordon Eustace. It was really too bad. Also, the mouse was getting all the titbits and the treats. The bear didn't like that either.

So the next time that there was a job to be done the bear decided to do it. He suddenly heard the golliwog say 'Hallo! The big red engine is very smeary. It wants a polish again. I'll go and call Sidney.'

Golly went to the mouse-hole and began to call down it. 'Sidney, Sidney, Sidney!'

But before the mouse could answer,

Sidney the bear rushed up to the golliwog. 'Yes! Did you call me? What do you want me to do?'

'Dear me – you're not as deaf as usual!' said the golliwog, surprised. 'Well, go and polish the red engine, then. You can have

a sweet out of the toy sweet shop if you do it properly.'

Sidney did do it properly. The golliwog came and looked at the engine and so did Amelia Jane. 'Very nice,' said Amelia. 'Give him a big sweet, Golly.'

The bear was pleased. Aha! He had done the mouse out of a job. The toys had been pleased with him, and the sweet was delicious.

And after that, dear me, you should have seen Sidney the bear rush up whenever his name was called. 'Yes, yes – here I am. What do you want me to do?'

Very soon the little mouse was not called up from the hole any more, and Sidney the bear worked hard and was friendly and sensible. The toys began to like him, and Sidney liked them too.

But one thing puzzled the golliwog and the big teddy bear, and they asked Amelia Jane about it.

'Amelia Jane – HOW did you know that

the mouse's name was Sidney Gordon
Eustace?'

'It isn't,' said Amelia with a grin.

'But it must be,' said the golliwog. 'He
always came when you called him by it.'

'I know – but he'd come if you called *any*
name down his hole,' said Amelia. 'Go and
call what name you like – he'll come! It's
the calling he answers, not the name! He
doesn't even know what names are!'

'Good gracious!' said the golliwog and
the bear, and they went to the mouse-hole.

'William!' called Golly, and up came
the mouse. He was given a crumb and went
down again.

'Polly-Wolly-Doodle!' shouted the big
bear, and up came the mouse for another
crumb.

'Boot-polish!' shouted Golly, and up
came the mouse.

'Tomato soup!' cried the big bear. And
it didn't matter what name was yelled
down the hole, the mouse always came up.

He came because he heard a loud shout, that was all. Amelia Jane went off into fits of laughter when the mouse came up at different calls. 'Penny stamp! Cough-drop! Sid-Sid-Sid! Dickory-Dock! Rub-a-dub-dub!'

The mouse's nose appeared at the hole each time. How the toys laughed – all except Sidney the bear!

He didn't laugh. He felt very silly indeed. Oh, dear – what a trick Amelia Jane had played on him! But suddenly he began to laugh, too. 'It's funny,' he cried. 'It's funny!'

It certainly was. Amelia *would* think of a good idea like that, wouldn't she?

5 Amelia Jane is very busy

One day Amelia Jane sat very still in her little chair, and watched somebody knitting in the playroom. It was little Miss Jones, who came to help with the children's clothes. She was knitting a jersey for the biggest boy.

'Click-click-clickity-click!' Her knitting needles flashed in and out all day long, and Amelia Jane watched and watched.

When little Miss Jones had finished all the knitting and had put the balls of left-over wool neatly in the work-basket with the long needles, she left the playroom to go home.

As soon as she had gone Amelia Jane ran to the work-basket. She took up two needles and a ball of wool and went to sit on the rug by herself, leaning against the table-leg.

'I can knit,' she told the toys. 'I know how to. I watched Miss Jones all day long. You go like this – and like that – and see, the knitting comes!'

The toys watched her. They thought

Amelia Jane was very clever. Click-click-clickity-click – why, her needles went as fast as Miss Jones' needles!

'What are you making?' asked the sailor doll.

'Nothing. I'm just knitting,' said Amelia.

'But you must be knitting *something*,' said the clockwork mouse. 'You can't just *knit*.'

'It's a waste of wool not to make some-thing when you knit,' said the teddy bear. 'Can't you make me a jersey?'

'No. It would take me ages to knit a jersey to go over your fat little tummy,' said Amelia Jane.

'Don't be rude,' said the bear, offended. 'If *you* kept a growl in your tummy, you'd be fat, too. Grrrr!'

'Couldn't you knit me a bonnet?' said the baby doll. 'I could do with a new one.'

'No, I couldn't. You've got three al-ready,' said Amelia Jane. 'For goodness' sake go away and let me *knit*! I tell you,

59

I'm not making anything at all, I'm just knitting.'

The baby doll sat down by her and took off her hair-ribbon to smooth it out. She was very particular about her ribbons. She put it down beside her, and began to comb out her hair with a little comb.

'Go away,' said Amelia. 'I don't like people who comb hair all over me.'

'Well, you can just put up with it,' said the baby doll, crossly. 'I can sit where I like.'

Amelia Jane didn't say anything – but when the baby doll looked for her hair-ribbon it had gone!

'You've taken it!' she said to Amelia. 'You mean thing. Give it me back.'

'She can't. She's knitted it with the wool!' said the golliwog, pointing. And sure enough that bad Amelia Jane had taken the ribbon and knitted it – and there was the ribbon, right in the very middle of the knitting.

'I can't take it out,' said Amelia. 'It would spoil my beautiful knitting. You'll have to do without your ribbon now. It's your own fault.'

The baby doll went off, crying. 'Cry-baby!' said Amelia Jane, and went on knitting.

'Your knitting is nothing but a long, long scarf, very narrow,' said the bear. 'It's silly knitting. Nobody would wear a scarf like that.'

'Nobody's going to,' said Amelia Jane. 'I wish you would stop bothering me. Can't I knit if I want to?'

'The click-click noise makes me cross,' said the sailor doll.

'It doesn't take much to make you cross,' said Amelia. 'Clockwork mouse, what do *you* want? Don't you dare to nibble my wool!'

'I just want to watch you knit,' said the mouse, and he sat down close by. And will you believe it, that rascally Amelia Jane knitted his long tail into her knitting! The little mouse suddenly found himself pulled towards Amelia's knitting, and saw his tail there!

Goodness, what a to-do there was! The bear was very angry. 'You can't do things like this, Amelia!' he said.

'I can,' she said. 'And I have. The mouse can't have his tail back. It belongs to my knitting now.'

But the sailor doll made her undo the tail because the clockwork mouse was so upset.

'He can't hang on to your knitting by his tail,' he told Amelia Jane. 'You're very unkind and very silly. Just *look* at the enormous length of knitting you have done – all for nothing, too!'

The next thing he knew was that Amelia had pulled out his bootlaces and had knitted those, too! She wouldn't give them back, either, and the sailor doll stamped round the nursery in a rage, his boots slipping off his feet every minute!

'She'll have to fall asleep sometime soon,' whispered the teddy bear to the golliwog. 'Then we'll pay her out for all this!'

So they waited till her needles worked more and more slowly – clickity-click, clickity-click – click – click – – click – – – click – and then they stopped. Amelia Jane was fast asleep!

The toys crept up to her. They took up the long, long strip of knitting. They wound it all round Amelia Jane and the table-leg she was leaning against – round and round and round and round!

'Now she's all tied up in her own knit-ting!' said the golliwog, pleased. 'And the more she knits, the more tied up she will get.'

Amelia Jane woke up merry and bright. She picked up her knitting needles and started off again – clickity-click, clickity-click!

But soon she found that she was bound tightly to the table-leg, and the more she

pulled at her knitting, the tighter it became. She tried to stand up – but she couldn't.

'Oh! Oh! I've knitted myself to the table-leg!' she cried. 'Toys, help me!'

'Certainly *not*,' said the clockwork clown with a squeal of delight. 'Go on knitting. You'll soon be right in the middle of it and we shan't see you again! Knit hard, Amelia, knit hard!'

Amelia Jane didn't. She stopped. She tugged at the knitting to try to free herself but she couldn't. And dear me, how scared she got when she saw how the knitting was wound round and round and round herself and the table-leg!

'Undo me!' she begged the baby doll.

'I will if you knit me a new bonnet,' said the doll.

'Undo me!' Amelia Jane begged the bear.

'I will if you knit me a jersey and don't say anything about my fat little tummy,' said the bear.

'And you can knit me a red waist-coat,' said the golly.

'And me a new vest,' said the sailor doll.

'All right,' said Amelia. 'You're mean, all of you. But I'll knit what you want – and I hope nothing fits, so there!'

Well, they undid Amelia Jane from the table-leg, and then they helped her to pull undone all the long, long piece of knitting.

Out came the sailor's bootlaces and the baby doll's ribbon!

And then she had to set to work to keep her promises. She has made the bear a tight little red jersey.

'You'll never be able to get it off again, once you've got it on,' the golliwog told him, so the poor bear can't make up his mind whether to wear it or not.

Amelia has made the sailor a new vest, but as it reaches down to his feet he doesn't quite know what to do with it!

As for the golliwog's waistcoat, it's got three armholes instead of two! 'Use one for a leg!' said Amelia with a giggle. But how can he do that?

And now Amelia is knitting the bonnet for the baby doll, but as it is already big enough to go all round the teddy bear's middle, I expect she will have to use it for a shawl!

Can't you be sensible, Amelia Jane – just for once? Tie her up to the table-leg again, toys! She's just too bad for words.

6 Oh, bother Amelia Jane!

'What are you doing, Amelia Jane?' asked the sailor doll. 'What do you want that water for?'

'I'm going to paint,' said Amelia. 'See, I've found a paint-box in the toy cupboard. I know how to paint because I've watched the children.'

'How do you paint?' asked the sailor doll.

Amelia Jane dipped her paint-brush into the water and then rubbed it on one of the little squares of colour in the paint-box.

'I paint like this!' she said with a giggle and splashed a big stripe of green all across the sailor doll's face!

He was very angry. He went off to tell the other toys. 'She's in one of her silly moods again,' he said to the golliwog. 'We'd better look out!'

Amelia Jane painted hard all the morning. At first she painted pictures on a piece of paper. Then she looked round for something better to do with her paints.

'The dolls' house! I'll paint monkeys climbing up the wall,' she said. 'The little dolls have gone out for a walk – they'll be surprised when they come back!'

So she painted little brown monkeys all the way up the front walls of the pretty little dolls' house – they did look peculiar!

The dolls' house dolls screamed when they came back. 'Look! What's that on the walls? Monkeys! Are they real? Oh, what's happened to our dear little house?'

'You be careful in case there are monkeys inside it too!' said Amelia Jane, and not one of the tiny dolls dared to go in at their front door!

Then she saw the little wooden train standing by itself in a corner of the room.

69

The engine-driver had gone to talk to the teddy bear, so he wasn't there. Amelia Jane took her pot of water and paint-box – and do you know what she did? She painted rows of silly faces all round the engine and its trucks!

'Look! What's happened? Where did these dreadful faces come from?' cried the engine-driver when he saw them. 'My beautiful train! Everyone will laugh at me when I drive it.'

'You'd better get a cloth and rub all the faces off,' said the golliwog. 'Bother Amelia Jane! I'll help you, Engine Driver.'

So they spent a long, long time trying to get the faces off the engine and the train. They were very hot and tired by the end of it.

'I'd be much obliged if you would go and give Amelia Jane one good smack from me,' said the engine-driver. 'I'm too small to do it myself.'

'With pleasure,' said the golliwog, and he went up to Amelia Jane, and gave her one very good smack indeed. She was very angry – and you can guess what she did! She painted his black face white when he was asleep!

He did look queer.

He was very much upset. All the toys stood round him and giggled.

'Have you had a fright?' said the teddy

bear. 'You've gone very pale, Golly!'

He had to climb up to the little wash-basin, turn on a tap, put the plug in, and try to wash the white off his face. He managed to get himself wet all over, and the white ran down his coat and trousers.

So then he had to sit in front of the fire, and when his coat dried it shrank and was so tight that he could hardly breathe. He was very, very cross with Amelia Jane!

She painted the clockwork mouse's tail a bright red, and he thought it was a worm running after him. He raced away, squeal-ing. 'I can't get away from that red worm; it follows me, it follows me!' The toys couldn't help laughing.

'It's only your tail. Don't be afraid of your own tail,' said the bear. 'Go and climb up to the bookshelf, where the bowl of goldfish is. Sit on the edge and dip your tail into the water. The red will run off and you will be all right again.'

'Yes, you do that,' said Amelia Jane,

with a grin. *She* knew what would happen, but the others didn't! The clockwork mouse got up on to the bookcase, and went to the goldfish bowl. He sat on the edge and dipped his red tail into the water.

The goldfish were very excited. 'A worm! A lovely long red worm!' they bubbled to one another. 'Quick, catch it and eat it!'

And they swam to the little red tail and snapped at it. Goodness – the mouse almost fell backwards into the water! 'Don't! Don't! That's my tail!' he squealed.

He only just managed to get it out of the bowl before it was nibbled off. He raced down to the floor, tumbling over and over when he got there.

Amelia Jane laughed and laughed. The clockwork mouse cried bitterly. 'I wish *you* had a tail!' he said to Amelia Jane. 'I'd come and nibble it, then you'd know how it felt!'

Now the next night, a small mouse, a real one this time, came running out of a

73

hole in the playroom wall with a little note in his mouth. It was from the toys in the next house.

'I say!' said the clockwork clown, reading the note. 'The toys next door are giving a fancy dress party! What fun! It's the night after next. Well, I shall go as a pirate!'

'I shall go as one of the bears in the story of The Three Bears,' said the teddy bear.

'And I shall make myself a red cloak and hood and go as Red Riding Hood,' said the tiny doll in the corner of the toy cupboard.

'I shall go as a queen,' said Amelia Jane, grandly. 'I can easily make myself a crown, and there's a beautiful dress laid away in a box in one of the drawers over there. I can make a cloak, and I have got a very pretty necklace that came out of a cracker.'

Well, Amelia Jane worked very hard indeed at making the lovely cloak. It was royal purple and she sewed tiny silver beads all over it, from the bead box. She tried on her crown – how lovely she looked! She put on the necklace.

'Don't I look beautiful?' she said to the other toys. 'I shall win the first prize for the fancy dress. I know I shall!'

The golliwog thought she probably would. 'You don't deserve to,' he said. 'You've been unkind. The clockwork mouse is still upset because the red hasn't properly come off his tail.'

'Pooh!' said Amelia Jane. 'You wait till I get the paint-box out again. I'll do MUCH worse things than that!'

That made the toys very angry. The bear decided to take the paint-box and hide it when Amelia wasn't looking. It was quite easy to do that because she was so tired that night with her hard work sewing on the silver beads that she fell asleep!

'Look at her – fast asleep!' said Golly. 'She doesn't *deserve* to win the first prize at the party. But she will!'

'She won't,' said the bear, suddenly.

'I've got an idea, Golly. Listen – I can paint just as well as Amelia Jane can. And I'm going to paint her face in all kinds of stripes and dots while she's asleep! It'll be red and blue and green and yellow!'

The toys stood and giggled as the bear took the paint-brush, dipped it into the little pot of water, and began to paint Amelia's sleeping face. Goodness, he did it well! Stripes of red and green, dots of blue and yellow, crosses of black and brown.

Oh dear – what a terrifying sight Amelia Jane looked!

'But she'll see herself in the mirror, won't she?' said the clockwork mouse.

'No, because she would have to climb up on the bookcase, and stand there to see herself in the glass on the wall,' said the bear. 'And she won't do that when she's wearing a cloak. She couldn't climb in that.'

Well, when Amelia Jane woke up, she didn't know anything about her painted face, of course. All the toys put on fancy dresses for the party – and Amelia Jane couldn't *think* why they giggled every time they looked at her. In fact the clockwork mouse laughed so much that his key fell out.

Amelia walked up and down, wearing her crown and necklace, with the beautiful silk frock going 'swish-swish-swish' all the time, and her cloak flying out behind her, gleaming with silver beads. She didn't know how funny she looked with her painted face, all stripes and dots and crosses!

'First prize for *me*!' she said to the toys. 'Don't you think so?'

That made them giggle again, of course. Amelia Jane simply couldn't understand them. 'You're being very silly tonight,' she said. 'Well – I'm just going out into the passage to look at myself in the long mirror there. I don't want to climb up to the book-case mirror in this long cloak.'

The toys had quite forgotten *that* mirror! They wondered whatever Amelia Jane

would say when she saw herself. She walked out into the passage – and then she gave a loud scream.

'Oh! OH! My face! What's happened to it? Oh, you wicked bad toys, you've painted it! And I haven't time to wash it off properly. Oh, you horrid mean things.'

'We've only done to you what you did to us!' said the golliwog, grinning. 'You can't go to the party like that – and it serves you right!'

'I shall come! I shall! You just see!' cried Amelia Jane, and she took off her crown and her necklace and began to undo her cloak. 'Yes, and I'll get first prize, too! Oh, you unkind things!'

'Well, we won't wait. It's time we set off,' said the bear. 'Goodbye, Amelia Jane. We are sorry we shan't see you at the fancy dress party.'

But all the same Amelia is going! 'I look like a Red Indian, with war-paint on my face!' she thought, as she threw off her

lovely frock. 'All right – I'll go as a Red
Indian! Where's that little shuttle-cock
with coloured feathers set round it? They
will do for my hair!'

She pulled out the feathers and set them
round her head. Then she looked for the
little Indian wigwam tent that the bear
and golliwog sometimes played with. It
was painted gaily.

'That will do for a Red Indian cloak,'
said Amelia. 'And where's that rubber axe?

Ah, here it is – that shall be my tomahawk! And who shall be my enemies? The golliwog, the bear and all the rest! Look out – I'm coming to the party after all!'

And off she went at top speed, the fiercest Indian you ever saw. What a shock the toys are going to get! I can only hope that naughty Amelia Jane doesn't win the first prize after all!

7 Goodbye, Amelia Jane!

The toys played a trick on Amelia Jane the other day.

Amelia Jane was always playing tricks on all the toys in the nursery. There was no end to her mischief. If she didn't think of one thing, she thought of another.

There was the time when she collected worms in the garden and popped them all into the golliwog's shut umbrella. They wriggled about there and couldn't get out, poor things.

And then Amelia sent Golly out into the garden to fetch her hanky from the garden seat. It was raining, of course, so she gave him his umbrella.

'Better put this up,' she said, and he did.

And out slithered all the worms, on top of his head and down his neck, as soon as he got out into the garden in the rain.

The worms fled into holes very thankfully, but Golly got such a fright that he ran straight into the pond and got wet through.

He was very, very angry with Amelia Jane, but she only laughed.

'You shouldn't let worms nest in your umbrella,' she said.

Another time, Amelia took the teapot out of the toy tea-set and filled it with hot water from the tap. Then she climbed up to the roof of the dolls' house and poured the hot water down the chimney.

The little dolls' house dolls rushed out of the front door in fright, with water trickling down the stairs after them, and Amelia Jane nearly fell off the roof with laughing.

She was well scolded for that bit of mis-

chief, but she wouldn't even say she was sorry.

The toys had a meeting about her.

'I'm tired of Amelia Jane,' said the golliwog.

'So am I,' said the clockwork clown. 'She took my key away yesterday for about the fiftieth time.'

'Can't we get rid of her?' said the teddy bear.

'We've often tried,' said the clockwork mouse. 'But we never have.'

'I've got an idea,' said the golliwog, his black eyes shining brightly. 'It's a small idea at the moment – but if we talk about it, it might grow into a big one and be really good.'

'What is it? asked the clockwork clown.

'Well – you know you can slide down the stairs on a tray, don't you?' said the golliwog.

Everyone nodded.

'That's my idea,' said the golliwog. 'It's only just that. I haven't thought any more than that.'

'It seems rather silly,' said the bear. 'Did you mean to get Amelia Jane to slide down the stairs on a tray, or what?'

'I don't know,' said the golliwog. 'I tell you, I hadn't thought any further than I said.'

'Ooooh!' said the clown. '*Could* we make her slide down on a tray – push her very, very hard . . .?'

'And have the front door open so that she shot right out in a hurry,' went on the bear.

'And have the garden gate open so that she'd shoot out there, too,' said the clown.

'And then down the hill she'd go, whizz-bang, faster and faster and faster,' said the clockwork mouse, excitedly.

'And splash into the stream on her tray, and off it would go like a boat, all the way down to the sea!' finished the golliwog, his black face shining with excitement.

'And we'd never, never see her again, the bad, naughty doll,' said the bear.

'No, we wouldn't. We'd shout, 'Goodbye, Amelia Jane!' when she flew out of the front door, and that would be that,' said the golliwog. 'See what my little idea has grown to – a great big one. I thought it would!'

Well, the toys talked and talked about their idea, and got very excited about it indeed. Surely they could at last get rid of that naughty Amelia Jane!

she stared in fright. This was a much faster journey than she had imagined!

Down to the bottom of the stairs – along the hall at top speed – out of the open door – down the slippery front path – out of the open gate – and whooooosh – down the steep hill that led to the stream!

'Goodbye, Amelia Jane!' shouted the toys. 'Goodbye, goodbye!'

'She's gone,' said the bear, after a pause. 'Really gone. She'll never tease us again.'

'Never,' said the golliwog, pleased. 'She's played her last trick on us.'

'She deserved to be shot off like that,' said the clown. 'Now let's play at sliding trays downstairs all by ourselves.'

They played for quite a long time. Then they went back to the nursery to have a drink of water.

'I just hope Amelia Jane didn't tip off the tray going down the hill, and hurt herself,' said the bear, suddenly.

'And I just hope she didn't fall into

the stream and get drowned,' said the clown.

'It seems a bit funny without her,' said the mouse. 'Er – you don't suppose – we were dreadfully unkind, do you?'

'Not a bit,' said the golliwog. 'She deserved to be sent off like that.'

'But you wouldn't want her to hurt herself, would you? said the bear, solemnly. 'You know – I keep on and on thinking what would happen if she tipped off the tray going down-hill – suppose she fell under a horse's feet – or . . .'

The clockwork mouse gave a squeal of fright. 'Don't say things like that. They frighten me. You make me feel as if I want Amelia Jane back.'

'Perhaps she wasn't as bad as she seemed,' said the bear. 'You know – I don't feel very nice about playing that trick on her now. I feel sort of uncomfortable.'

'Pooh!' said the golliwog, but he didn't say any more.

Well, what *had* happened to Amelia Jane? She had slid out into the front garden and out of the gate, and down the hill at top speed. She was very frightened indeed. Why had the toys shouted goodbye? Was it a trick they had played on her to get rid of her? Amelia Jane wailed aloud as she shot down the hill. Oh, dear, oh, dear, had she been so dreadful that the toys wanted to get rid of her like that?

'I'm going straight into the stream!' she squealed, and splash, into the water she went. She clung to the tray. It didn't sink, but bobbed on the surface, with a very wet Amelia Jane clinging on top. Down the stream she went, bobbing on the waves.

She floated for a very long way. Then the tray bumped into the bank, stuck into some weeds and stopped. Amelia thankfully crawled off on to the land. She was wet and cold and tired. She could see a dog not far off and she was frightened of him.

Where could she hide? What was that

lying on the grass over there? A bicycle!
It had a basket behind the saddle, and
Amelia Jane staggered off to it. She
squeezed into the basket, and stuffed an
old bit of newspaper over herself. Now,
perhaps, nobody, not even the dog, would
see her.

She fell asleep and dreamed of the toys.
She dreamt that they were all cross with
her, and she cried in her sleep.

'Don't be cross with me. I'll be good, I'll be good.'

Then she woke up – and dear me, she was wobbling from side to side in the basket. Somebody had picked up the bicycle, mounted it, and was now riding away down the river path – with Amelia Jane tucked into the basket at the back.

'Oh, dear!' thought Amelia, in a panic. 'Now where am I going? I'm miles and miles away from home – and from all the toys. I wish I was back again. Wouldn't I be good if I could only get back to the nursery! But the toys wouldn't be pleased to see me at all. They'd turn me out again.'

On she went and on. Miles and miles it seemed to Amelia Jane, and she grew cramped and cold in the basket. And then, at last, the rider stopped and jumped off.

He flung his bicycle against something, and walked off, whistling.

Amelia Jane peeped out. The bicycle was against a wall near a back door. She crawled out of the basket, and almost fell to the ground. She ran to the door. If only she could get into a house, she could hide.

In she went, and somebody jumped up in surprise as the big doll ran past. Amelia tore into the hall and up the stairs. She almost fell inside a room, and stopped there, panting in fright.

And will you believe it, she was back in the nursery again – and there were all the toys she knew, staring at her in amazement – the golliwog, the bear, the clown, the mouse and everyone!

She had come all the way home in the basket of the bicycle belonging to the cook's little cousin! He had gone to the river that day, and then had cycled all the way to see the cook – and Amelia Jane was in his basket. What a very, very peculiar thing!

'You said goodbye to me – but here I am again,' said Amelia, in a funny, shaky sort of voice. 'It seems as if you c-c-c-can't get rid of me!'

She burst into tears – and then everyone ran to comfort her. She was patted and fussed, and even the golliwog kept saying he was glad to see her back.

'Oh, dear – this is all so nice,' said Amelia at last. 'I won't be mischievous again, toys. I won't play tricks any more. I'll be just as good as gold!'

'We don't believe you,' said the golliwog. 'But never mind – we're glad to have you back, you bad, naughty doll. We never *really* want to say goodbye to you, Amelia Jane!'

I don't either. What about you?

More Beaver Books

We hope you have enjoyed this Beaver Book. Here are some of the other titles:

The Wishing Chair Again Wouldn't you like a Wishing-Chair like Mollie and Peter have? They just sit in it and wish, and it flies them off to wonderful places like the land of Goodies and the Island of Surprises, where they meet Winks the naughty Brownie, Mr Spells the enchanter and a host of other lovable characters. Written by Enid Blyton and illustrated by Lesley Smith for younger readers

Wilberforce, Detective A funny and exciting story for younger readers in which Wilberforce the whale is called upon to protect the Crown Jewels! Written by Leslie Coleman and illustrated by John Laing

The Beaver Book of the Seaside A Beaver original. Snorkelling and surfing, birdwatching and beachcombing – plus facts about ships, lighthouses, smuggling, wrecks and lots of other fascinating topics. A book for everyone who loves the seaside by Jean Richardson; illustrated by Susan Neale and Peter Dennis

Over and Over Again A Beaver original. A superb collection of poems and songs, old and new, for the very youngest children, compiled by Barbara Ireson and Christopher Rowe and illustrated by Russell Coulson

New Beavers are published every month and if you would like the *Beaver Bulletin* – which gives all the details – please send a large stamped addressed envelope to:

Beaver Bulletin
The Hamlyn Group
Astronaut House
Feltham
Middlesex TW14 9AR

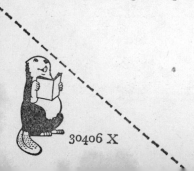

30406 X